CONTENTS

ACKNOWLEDGMENTS

Kindle Direct Publishing is Amazon.com's e-book publishing unit launched in November 2007, concurrently with the first Amazon Kindle device.
Copyright @ Abdullah-al-Musa
All right reserved ISBN: 9798643463771
Imprint: Independently published
This is a work of friction, names , characters and incidents are either the product of author's imagination or are used fictitiously , and resemblance to any actual person, living or dead, events or locales is entirely coincidental. But the description of places is author's own experience .

Graphic design : Abdullah-Al-Musa .

CHAPTER 1

Before the journey to Malaysia I have heard that Kelantan is the 'Land of Lighting', an overwhelmingly rural state with a relatively short coastline and only one major urban . Many people things that Malaysia has it all for the perfect vacation . Traveler's find a wealth of attractions, from the world's oldest rainforests and sun-kissed island to historical cities and cultural treasures , right here in the heart of Asia .

My friend Mehbub said to me , 'When you write about your adventure of your PhD study you must start with this and must think this is a puzzle to you.'Mehbub Anowar a drama actor singing the song-

> Sitting there absent mindedly
>
> Grazing vacantly toward the sky
>
> I will bring for you
>
> Rain from the sky with blazing wind
>
> The wind will take you away

It has been written by Mehbub favorite poet S.R Matin. With the funny tone I replied 'It's true that we don't know what we've got until we find it, but it's also true that we don't know what we've been finding until it arrives.'

Actually I didn't know the puzzle until I actually start my Research work at UMK .

Then Mehbub said 'I know . But this is just a technique , to tickle the fancy of the reader .'

As a matter of fact I was not happy with this answer .Mehbub Anowar realized it , so a couple of minutes later , he added ' Anyone who reads that puzzle at the outset will get the chance to use his own intelligence , you see.'

So , I agreed to start my PhD journey story with it . I should , however , point out at once that it's no use trying to work out what it means . It's not easy at all . In fact , it took even quite a long time to discover its meaning , although when I eventually understand , it seemed simple enough , but it is not a puzzle at all , it was an inspiring song.

The story began in Dhaka . It was Sunday , 7 August. The time was 10.30 a.m. of late , the maximum temperature had hit 97.0 Degree of Fahrenheit, so I was keeping myself indoors   , pasting old National Geographic magazine from Nilkhet market near to New Market and spending time alone . However I had recently finished my Master's Degree. At this moment I was resting at home , stretched out on a divan , smoking a cigarette and reading TinTin's *The Crab with the Golden Claws*. A minute later , my friend Mehbub turned up .

Mehbub Anowar Tufan –the successful drama actor of immensely popular TV drama ,film as well as stage actor , had started visiting me at least twice a month . The popularity of his stage drama performance meant that he was pretty well off . As a matter of fact , he was once rather proud of his state drama performance .

But when I pointed out dozens of factual errors in his performance , Mehbub began to look upon me with a mixture of respect and admiration . Now , he got his idea of new drama performance so he came for correctness.

Today , however , he was carrying a sheaf of papers under his arm , which clearly meant that he was a different reason for his visit . He sat down on a sofa , took out a green face towel from his pocket , wiped his face with it , and said without looking at me , ' Would you like to do your PhD in the 'Land of Lighting', Rashed ?'

I raised myself a little , leaning on my elbow. 'What is your definition of Land of Lighting?'

'The same as yours, Rashed. Where sun is shine in the cluster of trees . Dense foliage . That sort of things .'

'In country or abroad?'

'In abroad.'

'Is it Malaysia ?'

The reason of saying Malaysia –is that I was thinking about to start my PhD .

'Yes Sir.'

'Where in Malaysia ? I can not think of any place other than Langkawi or Johor Bharu .

'Have you heard of University Malaysia Kelantan?'

The questions was accompanied by a rather smug smile . I had heard about the University Malaysia Kelantan is a public university in kelantan.

The formation of the university was mooted during the tabling of the Ninth Malaysia Plan and approved by the cabinet of Malaysia on 14 June 2006 . The launching ceremony was held at the end of 2006 by Prime Minister , Y.A.B .Tun Abdullah Ahmed Badawi . The first students were enrolled with the commencement of the June 2007 semester .'Oh? You mean that you have some news about this university ?

The answer was accompanied by a rather smug smile .'Doesn't this land sharing border with Thailand?'Mehbub asked.

'Yes , Sir ', I replied , 'Entering the Tumpat district , west of the capital , and you would thinking that you are already into Thailand .'

'Yes , Sir ', I replied , 'Entering the Tumpat district , west of the capital , and you would thinking that you are already into Thailand .'

Actually the letter he had got , when he entering my house . Probably post master just drop it on the floor . And I was waiting for a long time to get this letter . This was nothing but my scholarship accepting letter as a PhD researcher in University Malaysia Kelantan.

Malaysia is located in Southeast Asia . Land border's with Thailand, Indonesia , Brunei and maritime border are shaped with Singapore, Philippines and Vietnam. The capital of Malaysia is Kuala Lumpur while Purtrajaya is the federal administrative center of the country. Malaysia comprises of 14 states, each state is headed by a sultan or head of the state.

'So , you have you heard of University Malaysia Kelantan (UMK)? I asked the question , opening the envelope by a rather smug smile . I know he had heard of this , too .

'Does it your scholarship letter , or it is only your admission letter?' Mebbub asked .

'Yes , Boss', I replied , taking out the letter from the envelope with a flourish smile.

University Malaysia Kelantan , the autonomous public institution of higher learning in the state of Kelantan , was established with the core business of entrepreneurship education. Therefore, UMK adopts the philosophy "Entrepreneurial University".

'Why, Mehbub, why did you think something else , a love letter?' I asked him with a smile.

'What! that means this is your scholarship letter from UMK?' Mehbub asked , looking with joy, ' I didn't know . I mean .....there hasn't been any news from UMK for a long time , and they may forget about you . So I thought perhaps .....' His voice with excitement. 'Well, you see, Rashed, I had read a book -The journey of Malaysia a few days ago. In fact, he added with a smile , ' I am thinking myself to go Malaysia as a tourist. Again he said 'So, you did success?'

I showed him the letter from the envelope .'Yes , UMK wouldn't send this scholarship letter , would they ?'
' Well , you are success , Mehbub said with smile.

The city campus is located in 10-15 minutes to kota Bharu(the capital city of Kelantan) and 5 minute drive to Sultan Ismail Petra Airport . The enrollment of students in city campus is around 1200. It houses the Center of post graduation studies . The campus is located in strategic area which are surrounded by food stalls, a 24-hours. McDonald outlet , launderettes , book store and a hypermarket.

It came as no surprise to me that Mehbub liked about my study at UMK so readily . Actually my own heart was jumping with joy when I have got the scholarship letter . The fact was that my sister was a Doctor as well . Our central home was in the village of Dogachi , near Pabna Sodor. My late father was the eldest son . He worked in the public works department as a civil engineer. He was renowned in the area of making lots of government building in Dhaka as well as other district in Bangladesh . However, that did not stop him from being terrific at sports .

Mehbub himself has always been fascinated by recite poem. He has read every book written by S.R Matin. Although he's never been wrote any poem , he did learn to recite poem and is now a top person in this area . There is no doubt in my mind that he could easily write poem , should he be required to do so. He has often told me S.R Matin's lyric poem open his thinking . Even the simplest of word he described was more interesting , therefore, no different that he is his best poet .

' What is strange ' , he continues, ' that although this are his sixth book –and he began writing at the age of forty –it reads as though it's been written by an experienced writer . He has a wonderful style. He probably turned to writing when he was travelling in Europe ,' Mehbub remarked. ' May other writer has agreed that he is a skilful writer. His language is wonderful .Perhaps its something to do with being close to nature. Think of the sages who wrote the scriptures .'

In talking about this experience , I have so far thought to used real names and real places . But this time , I have been thought myself not to do so .

I had turn to Mehbub for advice on fictitious names I might use . 'You can mention the place name and description there's no problem in that ,' Mehbub said , ' but you can change the character name as fictitious but you can give the real description of places .'

The chief character might be called Prof Dr. Yousuf Bin Youhan . He was an amazing researcher , supervisor and teacher . In fact , he was professional , meticulous, human and makes every effort to support his student. The door to his office was always open whenever I ran into a trouble spot or had a question about my research writing .

I am doing what Mehbub told me to do . The names of people are fictitious as well as events , but not the place. I shall try to relate everything exactly as I saw or heard it .

CHAPTER 2

'**W**ill you stay at home ' said Mehbub Anowar . 'You have to start doing your necessary market for your journey'. Then in an admiring tone he said again 'No where in the country you will find everything expect New Market and day before yesterday I had a shooting at Nasirullah's Phuchka and Chatpati shop !'.

New Market is one of the most famous and old market in Dhaka city . It was established in 1958 by Dhaka city corporation. It is a two stored building within a triangular shape .

The center of New Market has a beautiful mosque surrounded by shops selling home and family products , sari , clothes , shoes , books , stationary , jewelry , fast food , electronic products and kitchen products . New Market has three big gates and is almost twenty five acres in area.

I was in full agreement .We were now standing opposite of New Market , having just seen Spiderman from Bolaka Cineplex . This is one of the old and famous cinema hall in Dhaka . It was built in the early 1960 s . Situated in opposite of New Market area , beside Neelkhat and Bakusha Books market . Bolaka Cineplex hall on the right side of Mirpur road , going through Mirpur road from Eden College side .

Mehbub needed mobile charger for his mobile and refill for his ball point pen . I wanted to eat Phuchka and Chatpati from Nasirullah's shop . Though this foods are not local of Bengal , it traveled with the non-Bengali working and business community from the northern states of India settled in and around Kolkata in late 19th century . The name 'Phuchka' was given in Bengal perhaps from the sound "fooch" that the crispy fired ball makes when pressed by thumb to make cavity for filling potato-mix stuff and 'chutney' water. Besides, Mehbub wanted to go around the whole market . 'Only day before yesterday ' you see , I did a new TV drama shoot right here in Nasirullah's shop!' he told me.

We stepped into the traffic to cross the road , making our way carefully through endless private cars and taxies . Mehbub began to give me details story of new TV drama . ' The main actor of this drama is me , act as a police officer who has always thinking whether his investigation is right or not , so one day this police officer comes to this New Market when it is nearly closed , so he could not find an exit . Every dark corridor is empty , except for Nasirullah's shop in a small narrow alley . There is only a flickering light in this shop . He run towards the shop in the hope of finding help. Just as he reach it , a man comes out of the darkness .

He said to the police officer 'what do you want to eat , sir?' Officer was sweating . The seller boy said, 'please sit down.' After a few minutes he gave the police officer Phuchka and Chatpati . But when he serves the officer comprehends , an arm comes out of the darkness.

It is the arm of a skeleton , a dragger clutched in his other hand , dripping with blood . It is the skeleton of the seller boy . No matter how fast he runs or where he goes , he could still see the skeleton's arms , getting closer ... and closer .'

'No where in the country you will find everything expect New Market and day before yesterday I had a shooting at Nasirullah's Phuchka and Chatpati shop !'.

Not bad , I thought quietly to myself , an idea like this certainly had possibilities .

We were by now central of New Market . In front of us was a shop selling mobile goods . Mehbub could buy his mobile charger there and a refill for his pen from the shop opposite . The owner of Alif Electricals and Mobile knew Mehbub . He greeted us with a smile . We were followed almost immediately by other man —about forty years of age , medium height bush shirt and black trousers . In his hand was a plastic bag .

'Rakib Biswas!' when Mehbub's elder brother went to visit Malaysia , Rakib Biswas arranged all his papers . Actually he was working in Malaysian hi-commission at Dhaka .'Why this is Mehbub Anowar !'

'What a coincidence , you know , this is my friend Rashed , he got admission in a Malaysian University , so he needs your help to submit papers in Malaysian hi-commission at Dhaka. '

'Congratulation , that's not a problem at all to submit papers .'Said Rakib Biswas cleared his throat . He said again , 'will you please give me your mobile number , so I could give you mine , then you could send your address .'

I said to him , let's go to the Zhal-Muri shop , so Rakib Biswas and I came to the Zhal-Muri Shop . Rakib Biswas put his hand into his pocket and take out his mobile phone and take my number .

Meanwhile Mehbub had gone to buy refill for pen . He returned just as Rakib Biswas left .

'Have you gave your detailed to Mr Rakib Biswas ?' he asked . I smiled , but did not say anything . We were near to the Zhal-Muri shop . I was in silence , looking straight ahead , but my eyes and ears were taking in every detail. As usual the market was very crowed today. Mehbub said something about the crowd 'Cosmopolitan'. But could not ask him to repeat what he had said , for we were now at the Zhal-Muri shop .

Dhaka is the capital and largest city of Bangladesh . It is the largest city by population in the historical region of Bengal and a major city in South Asia . Dhaka emerged as a cosmopolitan city during the Mugal Empire . It is a hub for trade and culture , with a long history as a Bengali Capital . It has been called the city of Mosques and the Venice of the East, due to its Islamic architecture and riverfront facing the Buriganaga (old Ganges) . It is also known as the Rickshaw capital of the world , as there are over 500,000 cycle rickshaws running on its roads. Although it is described as a concrete jungle . Dhaka has venerable green spaces , including many gardens and parks . Today's Dhaka is South Asia's second most populous capital after Delhi and important financial center alongside Mumbai and Karachi .

'Assalamualuikum wbt Sir ' said the Zhal-Muri owner and began making up a packet for us .

He knew what we wanted . I love watching the way he mixed all the masala with muri , shaking the packet gently . It contents , I knew , would taste heavenly to me.

He finished in a few moments and passed the Zhal-Muri packet to me and then after a few minutes another Zhal-Muri packet to Mehbub.

I put my hand into my pocket to take out my wallet and turned into a statue.

Mehbub noticed it and said 'What on earth the matter ? What are you seeing? Have your wallet been stolen ?'It took Mehbub a moment to realize what it was . My wallet's was quite safe , but I was looking around to find out Rakib Biswas , who had just dropped this paper .

I found a paper with printed word had been cut of books or newspapers and pasted on a sheet of paper near to the Zhal-Muri shop , where few minutes ago Rakib Biswas was standing.

It must be fall down when he take out his mobile from his pocket. I picked it up . It said *'Be papered to pay for your sins '*, I read it .

'Mysterious piece of paper, ' whispered Mehbub Anowar. I felt inclined to agree with him.

'There's nothing to feel like this , really ,'I remarked . 'So what if this is someone .' Dozens of people around here !'

I had notice lighting ripping the sky soon after we left New Market . By the time we reached the bus station to go back to Mirpur , it was half past seven o'clock . And there was frequent thunder .However , when we alighted at New Market in the evening , there was no evidence of sudden rain .

CHAPTER 3

'**No** Sir ,' said Mehbub Anowar most emphatically , ' If a sea doesn't surrounded a land , then I don't want to suggest you to go for study. '

Probably this inspiration he got from S.R Matin poem . But I understand what he is implying about . He is thinking about Kelantan .

Kelantan is positioned in the north-east of Peninsular Malaysia . It is bordered by Narathiwat Province of Thailand to the north , Terengganu to the south-east , Perak to the west and Pahang to the south . To the north-east of Kelantan is the South China Sea .

He was sitting in my living room the next evening , talking idly about my going to Kelantan for PhD Research . There was an atlas lying on a coffee table .Mehbub Anowar stretched out a hand towards it , possibly to find the map of Malaysia , but withdraw it as the bell rang. I answered the door and a minute later , Mr Rakib Biswas walked in to collect my passport for the immigration from Malaysian Hi-commission at Dhaka .

I went to the kitchen to made some tea , only a few moments later, I came with a cup of tea and my passport with other UMK related document .

' Is this your note ?' I asked as soon as I put the tea cup on the table . Rakib Biswas eyebrows shot up immediately and his mouth fell open .

'Let me explain , ' I lit a cigarette and said , we saw this note soon after we met you yesterday in New Market.''Mr Rashed!' Mr Rakib cried , bringing his fist down on the arm of his chair in excitement .' it came by post . I have no idea , why it is coming to me.'

I have no idea , why it is coming to me.

'Well, -then? Where do you live ?'

Rabik Biswas said with the same tone '172 Lalbagh Road.'

'We would like to visit your house one, if you don't mind.'

My eyes drooped . I remained silent . My eyes were now taking

in every detail of Lalbagh Area.

This time Mehbub said 'You know Rakib the job of a Researcher

can sometimes be almost like a detective. New piece of information,

like fresh clues , often shed a different light on events ha! ha! ha!'

'So you want to go my house to solve the mysterious threat

letter .' then a small pause he said that , Mr Rashed , these few days

I am feeling more disturbed , because of this threat letter , you see

, I had taken another five letter . Look!

It is the same paper cutting said *Be papered to pay for your sins.'*

Rabik Biswas remained silent for a while after he had

finished tea . Then he frowned and said , 'You mean you think you

need to do investigate?'

Why , didn't you tell me you were disturbed by looking this

mysterious letter ?And you said you read it so many times and thinks

a lot but could not figure it out yourself !'

'Yes , that's true Mr Rashed , I will be much happy if you solved this .'

'All right , first we want to visit your house , 172 Lalbagh Road.'

Just after then Mr Rakib left , Mehbub said 'Incredible ! , your Phd research would help you to solve other mystery.'

'Yes .Anyway , I think we should go and visit Mr Rakib Biaswas house.'

To my amazement just after two days, Mr Rakib text me , to collect my passport from his house .

We went in through the old city of Dhaka was small centering round Babubazar area, but on becoming the capital of the Mughal Subah the city was extended along the bank of the Buriganga river.

Mehbub said to me , ' The capital requirements led to expansion of the city. Localities grew in different locations in light of the professional occupation of people. If you noticed the names, which persist even today, suggest how the city grew and developed. Urdu Road suggests the camp of soldiers, Bakhshibazar, Mughaltoli, Hazaribagh, Peelkhana, Amligola, Atishkhana, Mahouttoli, Bongsal, Kayettoli, Tantibazar, Sankharibazar, Ganaktoli, all signify that they had been occupied and inhabited by Mughal civil and military officials and their retinue at one time or another.'

'What do you think the important things in the mysterious letter business?' he asked.

'Smell of rose.' I replied.

After that Mehbub stop asking me another question. But again he started to say , ' In Lalbagh, the construction of the only fort in Dhaka, the Lalbagh or Aurangabad fort was undertaken in 1678-79. It was an incomplete fort as Subehdar Shaista Khan did not continue the work once his daughter Paribibi died.

The Mughals developed the area adjunct to it. Chandnighat on the river Buriganga, half km east of Fort, was developed as a landing station and for review of imperial war-boats. Chawk, the market place and Katra were built further east of it. Lalbagh Shahi Mosque the largest Mosque in Bangladesh was built few yards away from the south east corner of the Fort. Amirgola and Nawabganj, west of the Fort was the residential area for the officers and nobles attached to the Fort. Atiskhana area, as the name suggests, a place for storing ammunition and explosives, was located half km north west of the

Fort and Peelkhana, further west, was the stable for Elephants. Azimpur area north of the Fort was also a residential place for nobles. The decline of Mughal power and rise of the East India Company in the 18th century led to the waning of the importance of Dhaka and its population began to dwindle sharply. Lalbagh Fort and its surroundings soon became forlorn and desolate.

The city attracted British, Dutch, Portuguese and Armenians traders. They established factories at Tejgaon and Narinda area. Amirgola, Hazaribagh and Posta in Lalbagh transformed into places for small local industries for making comb and buttons from Buffalo horns and tanneries etc. Hindu traders gradually settled in there. They were Poddars and Baniks. It is said the Bank of a famous banker 'Jagat Seth' was located close to 'KillarMor' (south west corner of Fort) beside anopen field and temple. In 19th century, the houses of Dhaka were mostly thatched huts erected in a line upon the edges of narrow winding streets and alleys. Dhaka land was not level, houses were clustered on the high strips of land lying between creeks and canal branches. In 1844, the British brought the convicts at Lalbagh Fort for its maintenance and in 1853 the Army was moved in from Paltan to stay. During Sepoy mutiny of 1857 the local troops revolted which was brutally crushed.

Many sepoys were killed, many were arrested and executed at Victoria Park. Meanwhile, valuables of the Fort, stones and costly sandalwood items of Paribibi's tomb were looted. The Fort thereafter was used as a police barrack till the partition of India 1947.After partition, another tragic event took place in Lalbagh Fort in 1948, when the police stationed there refused to take orders or lay down arms due to long non-payment of salaries and allowances.

When negotiations failed, army was called in to crush rebellion. EP Rifles from Peelkhana surrounded the fort from all sides in the morning and army regiment moved in the Fort to disarm them. Thousands of people from near and far thronged the Fort area to witness the scene. Rooftop space of buildings and trees around the Fort were filled up and the open roads on north and south were packed with enthusiastic crowd. Gun battle took place in the afternoon and lasted for half an hour. Police surrendered taking heavy casualties, and Paribibi's tomb was splattered with blood. The crowd ran helter-skelter for their lives and many got injured in stampede and free fall from treetop. Years later, Police line from Lalbagh Fort was moved out to Mill-barracks and Rajarbagh.'

I was totally engrossed in what Mehbub Anowar was saying , and looking at the remains of the broken building , all built more then two hundred years ago.

We went in through the gate at 172 Lalbagh .I pressed the calling bell. Someone in the distance was talking to a mobile phone.

Mr Rakib opened the door and said 'please come in.'

We stepped into the living room. The house had a lovely old charm. Most of the furniture in the room was made of cane. We took two cane chairs . Just after a few minutes Mr Rakib came into the room with my passport and papers and said, ' now you are fully ready to go Malaysia for your study .'

But before he could say anything, one gentleman with clean saved and nearly six feet height walked into the room. Mr Rakib made the introduction, said 'Farid , happens to be my school friend . He works in Dubai .When I heard that he is coming from Dubai then I was going to let one of my rooms, otherwise he would have gone to a hotel.'

Mr Farid took a cane chair and lit the e-cigarette and laughed.' I did hesitate to take up his offer, I must admit ,chiefly because of my special weakness for e-cigarette . You see, Rakib might well have objected to the smell. So I wrote to let him know . He said he didn't mind, so here I am.'

'Are you here simply for a change of air?' Mehbub asked.

' Yes , but the air, I've noticed , isn't as cool and fresh as one might have expected.'

'Are you fond of smoking ?' I have asked unexpectedly.

' Yes , but how did you guess?' Mr Farid gave a startled smile.'

'Well , I noticed grey mark of your finger. I explained.'

' You're quite right,' Mr Farid laughed , 'this happen because of my long time addiction of e-cigarette.'

I have changed the subject .' Do you have another mysterious letter?' I asked to Mr Rakib.

'Oh yes, in my pocket,' said Mr. Rakib.

It was the same , not a hand written one. A few printer words had been cut out of books or newspapers and pasted on a sheet of paper .*Be prepare to pay your sins,*' it read.

' Have you reason to suspect anyone?'

'No. For the life of me, I cannot recall ever having harmed anyone.'

'Do certain people visit you regularly?'

Well , I don't get too many visitors . Recently I have got frequently internet problem .So , the line man comes occasionally if I happen to see any problem.'

'Are they good in their service?'

' About average , I should say. But then, my complaints have always been quite ordinary – I mean, no more than the weak internet connection.'

'Does they charge a fee?'

'Of course. But that's hardly a problem.'

'Who else visits you?'

'A Mr Gholam has recently started coming to my house.....look , here he is !' A man of medium height wearing a dark shirt was shown into the room.

'Did I hear my name?' he asked with a smile.

'yes, I was just about to tell these people that I have bought this cane furniture from your shop. Allow me to introduce them.'

After exchanging greetings ,Mr Gholam whose full name was

Gholam Shovon Saworar said to us , ' I thought I'd drop by since you didn't come to the shop today.'

' N-no , I wasn't feeling very well. So I decided to stay in.'

It was clear that Mr Rakib did not want to tell Mr Shovon about the letter. I had hidden in the minute Mr. Shovon had walked in.

'All right, if you're busy today. I'll come back another time....actually, I get it for you.'

Mr Rakib disappeared into the house to fetch other letter.

'Do your house here in Old Dhaka ?'I asked to Mr Farid .

'No,' he replied. I don't stay in one place for very long .

Now I said to Mr Rakib , ' Don't you think it might be wise to go out of the house for the next few days?'

'Yes, you're probably right. But this business of an anonymous letter is so incredible that I cannot really bring myself to take seriously. It just seems like a foolish practical joke!'

'Well why don't you stay in until we can be definite about that ? How long have you had that servant?'

'Right from the start. He is completely reliable.'

I now turned to Mr Farid. ' Do you stay at home most of the time?'

'Yes, but I go for morning and evening walks, so I am out of the house of a couple of hours everyday. In any case, should there be any real danger, I doubt if I could do anything to help.'

' Don't involve poor Farid in this , please ,' Mr Rakib said, ' After all, he's here from Dubai to get some relax, so let him enjoy himself. I'll stay in if you insist, together with my servant. You two can come and visit me . But since you get's your all paper , so I think you should better go to your university and settle down in study .

' Yes , you are right .'

I stood up . So did Mehbub . It was time to go.

There was a group football team picture in front of us. Over it , on a bookshelf were one framed photographs. I moved closer to look at these.

'This is my school day football team photo,' said Mr Rakib with a short smile.'

Mr Farid began laughing .' That photo is there simply to show how time can change everything. Would you believe that is our own football team photograph taken, that is my own photograph , and this is Rakib , taken when we were in the same school. We used to go to a missionary school in old Dhaka in those days. My father was

the magistrate there .

But I must say ,Rakib was extremely naughty. Our teacher were

all fed up with him. In fact, he didn't spare the students , either,

he was our team captain . I remember him having kicked the

best runner in our school in a hundred - yard race to stop him

from winning.'

We started walking towards the front door.

'A very interesting case, but I have solved your problem Mr

Rakib , just you do a little favor of me, tell me which air line I will

take to go Kota Bharu?' I asked.

'oh, really you solved the mysterious letter matter ? said Mr

Rakib.

' I will tell you , please buy a ticket for me and tell me the price ,

I will transfer the money and meet me tomorrow.' I said.

' Now you are talking like the detective one , That's not a matter

, one of my friend work in Air Asia. So he can arranged one for

you easily .'said Mr Rakib.

'Thank you. Goodbye!'

We came out of the house. It was already dark outside. Lights had been switched on in every house .Mehbub lingered. 'I am truly impressed by your power of observation,' he said , 'I too , have read a large number of detective novels. I found no clue this time . May be you can help me with this matter.'

'Really? But you said you didn't understand the matter?' ok , I saw you read all the letter , now take a smell of your hands.'

Mehbub now put his finger near to his nose , and muttered himself , 'Rose smell.'

'Look at the letter , I opened one letter , takes the various printed words. Do they tell you anything?'

Mehbub thought for a few seconds .' The words were cut out with a blade , not scissors, again this letter said nothing about money,' he said.

'Very good, but that was no need to ask openly.'

'Second, each word has come from a different source - the typeface and the quality of paper vary from each other.'

'Exactly, tell me, how did Mr Farid strike you today and who smoke Rose smell e-cigarette?'

'Mr Farid...yes I observed , he seemed little frightened.'

'Yes. Fear can make anyone nervous.'

'oh ? But why?'

'I would like the explanation from him , just wait until we meet Mr Rakib again.'

After then Mehbub keep remain silence , because we are now our bus stand.

CHAPTER 4

I stopped reading and shut the book with a bang . Then I snapped my fingers twice , yawned heavily and said , ' Social Engineering In Information Security .'

Mehbub asked , 'Were you reading a book on Social Engineering all this while ?'

The book was covered with newspaper , so he could not see its title. Recently I have bought this book from New Market , and took great care of it . As usual I put a protective cover of this book .

I lit a cigarette and blew out smoke and start talking , 'we have covered a lot of threats, but they have all been technological in nature. Social engineering deals with the targeting and manipulation of human beings with technology or other mechanisms. This method is popular because the human element is frequently the weakest part of a system and most prone to mistakes. If you watched the movies - *The Italian Job, and Matchstick Men* as great ways to observe different types of social engineering in action. *Catch Me If You Can* is a dramatization of the exploits of a real-life social engineer. If you watch these movies, pay close attention to the different ways social-engineering techniques can be employed, how they work, and why they are effective. A Wealth of Information in early 2017, Facebook officials announced that their user base had surpassed 900 million users, making it the largest social network of all time with further growth expected. Likewise, Twitter claims to have 8 million unique monthly visitors and 55 million monthly visitors. With this kind of volume and these network's inherent reach, it's easy to see why criminals look to these sites as a treasure trove of information and a great way to locate and identify victims. Not surprisingly, security stories about Twitter and Facebook have dominated the headlines in recent years. In one high-profile case, malicious person managed to hijack the Twitter accounts of more than 30 celebrities and organizations. They hacked accounts were then used to send malicious messages, many of them offensive. According to Twitter, the accounts were hijacked using the company's own internal support tools. Twitter has also had problems with worms, as well as spammers who open accounts and then post links that appear to be about popular topics but that actually link other malicious sites. Of course, Twitter isn't alone in this: Facebook, too, regularly chases down new scams and threats. Both sites have been criticized for their apparent lack of security, and both have made improvements in response to this criticism. Facebook, for example, now has an automated process for detecting issues in user's accounts that may indicate malware or malicious person attempts. With Facebook recently showing no signs of lessening in popularity, the issue of security will undoubtedly become higher profile. Over the next decade, more apps, services, and other technologies can be expected to switch to mechanisms that integrate more tightly with Facebook, using it as a sort of authentication mechanism. Although for the sake of convenience this may be a good idea, from a security standpoint it means that breaching a Facebook account can allow access to a wealth of linked information.

But I stopped talking as the bell rang . I answered the door and a minute later ,Mr Rakib Biswas walked in and sit on a chair.

'Mr. Rashed' ... he took a pause then said , 'the night passed peacefully and without any further excitement . In the morning , just as I sat down to have breakfast , but Farid did not come out , I went to his room and saw room is empty there was no bags of Farid , on the table I saw a letter.' said Mr Rakib.

With little embarrassment , he took out the letter with a trembling hand and passed it to me. 'You read it.' he said in a low voice.

I read it aloud. This is what it said :

Dear Biswas ,

When I first wrote to you from Dubai ,but before that our old school friend Mr Hasan told me you had a house in old Dhaka , I had no idea who you really were . But once I know it from Mr Hasan , then I understand you were none other than the boy who had once been my classmate in the missionary school in old Dhaka city at thirty years ago.

Anyway, when Mr Rashed came here , and the way he was asking question , so I understand he is a very clever man and he could understand the situation .

I did not know that the desire for revenge would raise my hand seven after so many years . You see , I was the boy you kicked at that hundred yards race on our sports day. Not only did I miss out on winning a medal and setting a new record , but you also managed to injure me pretty seriously. Since my father was magistrate , so he was transferred in Sirajgong district only a few days after this incident , which was why I never got the chance to have a showdown with you then ,never did you said sorry for it .

Never did you ever learn just how badly you had hurt me . I had to spend three weeks in a hospital with my leg .

When I heard from Mr Hasan that you were here, I suddenly thought of doing something that would cause you a great deal of anxiety and ruin your peace of mind, at least for a short time . This was my way of settling scores , and punishing you for your past sins. Unfortunately ,Mr Rashed understand whole incident . That is the reason I am leaving this place suddenly , soon I will go back to Dubai . But I hope you had got a little anxiety about the anonymity letter .

With good wishes,
Yours sincerely,
Farid

'So....tell me ....?' I closed the letter.

' My case of anonymity letter is solved . I don't want to go further this matter.' Mr Rakib grew his lopsided smile and continued, ' Here is your Air-Asia flight ticket and my account number , you can transfer the money by this account number . You will fly at 2nd September , reach to Kuala Lumpur airport , there one of my friend Mr Akash will wait for you . You will stay one day in his house , then next day you will have another flight to kota bharu , Sultan Ismail Petra Airport .'

'Thank you very much Mr Rakib.'

'You are welcome,' said MrRakib. Then he stood up.

'Aaah!' said Mehbub, sipping hot tea, his eyes half closed. 'that's totally solved everything.

We were decided that Mebhuh's uncle car would take and get to Hazrat Shahjalal International Airport .The Hazrat Shahjalal International Airport, is the largest and most prominent international airport in Bangladesh. It is located in Kurmitola 17 kilometres from the city center, in the northern part of the capital city Dhaka and it is also a part of BAF Bangabandhu Base used by the Bangladesh Air Force. The airport has an area of 1,981 acres. The Civil Aviation Authority of Bangladesh operates and maintains the airport. It started operations in 1980, taking over from Tejgaon Airport as the principal international airport of the country and was formerly known as Dacca International Airport and later as Zia International Airport, before being named in honour of Shah Jalal, who is one of the most respected Sufi saints of Bangladesh. However suddenly Mehbub's uncle driver has attacked of flu and fever at the last minute then Mehbub said, ' I think we would better take Ubbar car .'

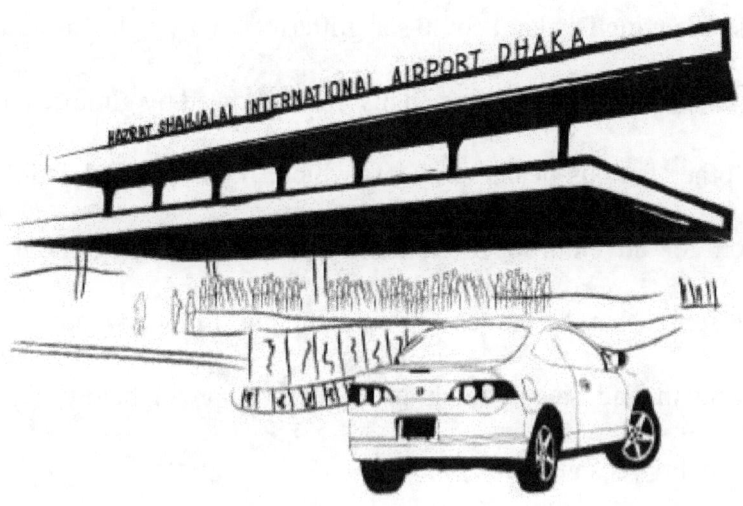

However suddenly Mehbub's uncle driver has attacked of flu and fever at the last minute then Mehbub said, ' I think we would better take Ubbar car .'

I agreed having Ubber car was a good idea , since we intended visiting a few other places. The officer who checked me in at the airport happened to know Mehbub. 'I'll give you seats on the right,' he said. 'You'll fell a good view.'

But I had no idea just how good the view could be. Within ten minutes of leaving Dhaka, I could see glittering on my right - a sight as rare as it was breathtaking. This was followed by glimpses of several other famous peaks, each of which, held an irresistible attraction for adventurous mountaineers. In less than three hours, I could sense that the plane was losing height. I looked out of the window again and saw a thick green carpet spread below. This must me palm trees garden.

At this point, disappeared into a grey mist and the plane started bumping up and down. Luckily, the mist cleared only a few minutes later, the plane steadied itself, and caught first glimpse of beautiful valley, bathed in sunlight.

CHAPTER 5

One doesn't have to be told this Malaysia is a foreign country!

True. I had never seen anything like this in Bangladesh. There were palm trees and rivers and green fields and big building- but, somehow, everything seemed different. Suddenly, it began to grow larger and larger, until it seemed to shoot up in the air and disappear. I had landed at Kuala Lumpur International Airport (KLIA).

The Kuala Lumpur International Airport is Malaysia's main international airport and one of the major airports in Southeast Asia and worldwide.

It is located in Sepang District of Selangor, approximately 45 kilometers south of Kuala Lumpur city center and serves the Greater Klang Valley conurbation.

I was scheduled to reach Kuala Lumpur in the morning at 10.45 a.m. The customs officials in KLIA were very strict. Apparently, every single passenger was required to have all his baggage examined. After then turned towards the exit.

It was my normal practice to get some reading done about any new place as was going to visit.

I had gone to Nilkhet bookshop day before yesterday and bought a book on Kuala Lumpur. I had leafed through it briefly, but what I saw in the glossy photos was enough to convince me that there could be few cities as lively and colorful as Kuala Lumpur.

Mr Akash was standing near the door, talking to a tall, white man with a beard. Since we made video whatsapp called .So , it was not difficult to know Mr Askah. His face broke into a smile as he caught sight of me. He said 'excuse me' to his companion and came forward to greet us.

'Welcome to Malaysia!' he said.

'Welcome to Malaysia!' he said.

'Thank you very much ,I felt I had to come.'

'Very good, very good.' Mr Akash shook my hand. Then he asked 'I suppose you would be here for a long time?'

'Three years or more than this. Where are you staying?'

'Cheras, Taman Connaught.'

'Tell me Mr Rashed , is this your first visit in Malaysia.'

'Yes , I said with side smile.'

It was seemed to me that Mr Akash has his own car . I have put all my language in the back of car , and sat beside Mr Akash . He stared the car , 'please tell me about Malaysia , I asked.' Mr Akash started talking , 'Do you know what is the meaning of Kuala Lumpur?

His face broke into a smile and said to me , 'ok, it means muddy confluence in Malay, kuala is the point where two rivers join together or an estuary, and lumpur means mud. Local people saying that it was named after Sungai Lumpur means muddy river. It was recorded in the 1820s that Sungei Lumpoor was the most important tin-producing settlement up the Klang River. Doubts however have been raised on such a derivation as Kuala Lumpur lies at the confluence of Gombak River and Klang River, therefore should rightly be named Kuala Gombak as the point where one river joins a larger one or the sea is its kuala. It has been argued by some that Sungai Lumpur is in fact Gombak River , therefore the point where it joined the Klang River would be Kuala Lumpur, although Sungai Lumpur is said to be another river joining the Klang River a mile upstream from the Gombak confluence, or perhaps located to the north of the Batu Caves area.

On my left were endless skyscrapers, but the sight of Petronas Twin Towers was visible from far away . Some were offices, others hotels. Each had shops on its ground floor, stacked from floor to ceiling with the most tempting objects. I came to realize later that the whole city was like a colossal departmental store. There was apparently nothing that you couldn't get in Kuala Lumpur.

A little later, we turned left and joined a high street. I had never seen anything like it before. A stream of humanity flowed down the pavement. The street was filled with buses, taxis, private cars. Both sides of the street were lined with shops. Their signboards hung so closely together that it was difficult to see the sky. Since Malay language is written horizontally, all the signboards hung in a horizontal line.

Our car moved slowly in the traffic, giving me the chance to take in everything. I had seen crowded streets in Dhaka enough times, but everyone there moved slowly, as if they had all the time in the world. Here, each person was in a hurry, trying to move as quickly as possible. Most of them were Chinese but Tamil and Malay people could be visible. From the way I saw some people carried their cameras, casting curious glances about them, it was easy to tell they were tourists.

At last, we came out of the high street and found ourselves in a relatively quiet area, on a street called Cheras Street. This was where Mr Akash lived, in a flat in a tall building with twenty-two floors. His flat was on the seventh.

We were getting out from the car. There was nothing we could do, anyway. So I followed Mr Akash in.

'Make yourselves comfortable,' Mr Akash said, accompanying me into his living room.

My wife and daughter are away—I took them back to Dhaka

only a few weeks ago to attend a niece's wedding—so please forgive me if there are lapses in my duties as host. What would you like to drink?'

'I think tea would be best, thank you.'

Mr Akash left to make the tea. I moved to the window to look at the view. Petronas Twin Towers was visible from the window. There was television in the room. A small table beside these was littered with various types of books. Mr Akash came in with the tea. He set the tray down, laughed. 'I heard from Rakib about the anonymous letter business . And I know you like adventure.'

'Yes , that was a very challenging things to solved the problem.'

'I would like you to meet with Prof Dr Mathew , he is from Mauritius. There's a very good restaurant just down the road. May be today I will take you some place, tomorrow I shall take you to airport , for your another flight to kotab haru!'said Mr Akash.

We were with the idea of going out for launch, when someone rattled the knocker on door. Mr Akash open it and said , ' Hello Dr Mathew. Allow me to introduce Mr Rashed .'

'Very good, very good.' Dr Mathew shook my hand with smile.

The gentleman who emerged from it was equally impressive, though that had nothing to do with his size. A man in his mid-fifties, he had a remarkably fair complexion and was wearing a fine shirt and gray trousers. On his feet were white shoes. And in his right hand he held a black shoulder bag, of a type which I had seen many times before.

We had lunch at Mydin restaurant. The food was heavenly.

'If you want to do any shopping, I suggest you do it now, although you may well have a little time tomorrow. Your flight isn't till 10p.m. , is it?' said Mr Akash.

'Tell me something about your country Dr Mathew?' I asked with smile.

'Well, officially called the Republic of Mauritius is an island nation in the Indian Ocean about 2,000 kilometers off the southeast coast of the African continent. The country includes the islands of Mauritius, Rodrigues, Agaléga and St. Brandon. Actually the islands of Mauritius and Rodrigues form part of the Mascarene Islands, along with nearby Réunion, a French overseas department. Well ,Mr Rashed, the reason I am here is only about this black shoulder bag .' said Dr Mathew.

Though his greying hair suggested he might be in his mid-fifties, but apart from that he seemed pretty well-preserved. There was a certain polish and sophistication in his voice and the way he spoke, but not even the slightest trace of arrogance . On the contrary, Dr Mathew spoke gently and quietly.

'I see. Allow me now to tell you why I'm here. You may find the whole thing totally insignificant. Anyway I have heard from Mr Akash , how you helped to his friend, so there's no way I can insist that you take the work. I can only make are quest.'

'Let's hear the details of your problem ,' I said.

Pointing at the black object in his hand .'Certainly you may called this my problem or the tale of exchange bag....ha! ha!ha!. Anyway recently I attended in a science symposium at Kota Bharu.'Said Dr Mathew with a smile I glanced at the black bag and said, 'It seems to me a new bag'.

'Yes, my bag was same size and look like it.'

'Your bag? You mean this one isn't yours?'

'No. This belongs to a person called Mr Khiruddin , he lives in kota bharu , even I heard about you from Mr Akash and he told me how you helped his friend about anonymous letter matter .'He took a pause and again said , ' I met with the gentleman in Air-Asia

flight, coming from kota bharu , he sat beside me , as usual we keep

our bag on the top , that time I did not noticed his bag , when I came

back home , then I discovered it .As he got my address in my

bag so Mr Khair uddin send my bag by post lagu . But I didn't

find any address in his bag. Unfortunately I am leaving KL today

, going to Mauritius for some family business . So I would like you

to send this bag to the address .Since you are going there tomorrow.'

CHAPTER 6

Kelantan is positioned in the north-east of Peninsular Malaysia. It is bordered by Narathiwat Province of Thailand to the north, Terengganu to the south-east, Perak to the west and Pahang to the south. To the north-east of Kelantan is the South China Sea.

Although the mist had lifted, the sky was still overcast, and it was raining. I didn't mind the rain. It was only a faint drizzle, the tiny raindrops breaking up into a thin, powdery haze. One didn't need an umbrella in rain like this; it was very refreshing.

The Sultan Ismail Petra Airport is located in Kota Bharu, Kelantan, Malaysia. Handling domestic flights to and from other parts of the country, the airport consists of one main terminal building. Inside the airport found some food store and shops. Luckily, on my right side I found taxi booking store. 'Since knowing nothing about the way to university, I'd better take a taxi.'

'Where to?'

'UMK campus hostel.'

I came out of the airport. Here, too, stood a row of different cars. I showed the taxi ticket and I got into one proton car. I was beginning to look upon these city with a new respect. It had taken exactly three minutes and fifty-seven seconds to reach to the university.

I couldn't help asking the question as we set off. 'Am I already to my destination?

'Yes, this is UMK city campus hostel,' said the driver. I am normally adaptable. I have seen my friend Mehbub remain perfectly unperturbed even under the most trying circumstances. If he had to spend a whole night at a railway station and the waiting room happened to be full, he'd quite happily stretch out on the platform. But there was one thing he couldn't do without that is reading in bed for a few hours before going to sleep.

Fortunately, I had my hostel room reservations. 'Your room is third floor,' said the hostel super.

I met my roommate Philip Lee . He was from Sarawak, but

he knew quite well the city .

I told him about the bag exchange business . Philip wanted to know the address .

2013-D kokpasir, Jalan Mutiara, Pengkalan Chepa.

'Ok it's not far from here.' Said Philip.

We went out after lunch. The main street outside our hostel was quite large. A number of buses, lorries and cars stood in the side of the road. On both sides were shops of various kinds. It was obvious that business people from almost every corner of Kelantan had come to Taman Bendahara. In many ways it was like University campus ,except that the number of people out on the streets was less, which helped keep the place both quiet and clean.

We had to reduced our speed we were in kok pasir, was trying to find 2013-dnumber house. Did man indeed live here? But no, the road we were travelling not broad at all, other cars had driven on the same road and, no doubt we were not alone.

The unmarred strange greenness ended abruptly about ten minutes later, with a black wooden board by the side of the road that proclaimed in black letters: 2013-dkokpasir,JalanMutiara,

Pengkalan Chepa. I had not expected our journey to end so peacefully. A little later we came upon a gate. Our car turned right and drove through the boundary. A long driveway led to a large, old-fashioned house , very obviously built a long time ago. A minute later, the owner of the house came out himself with an outstretched arm. Seeing the bag the gentleman may guessed everything .

'Hello , I am Rashed and this is my friend Philip, we are here to give this bag , is this your bag that exchange in Air Asia, with a man called Dr Mathew ?

'Yes this is mine, I was lucky I got his address in his bag. With a pause he said , allow me to introduce myself , I am Khairuddin.'

I handed over the black bag before sat down. The smile on Mr Khairuddin's face did not falter.

'Please check the contents in your bag,' I said with a slight smile.

'If you say so,' replied Mr Khairuddin, laughing, and opened the bag.

Then he ran his eyes over the items and said, 'Yes,

everything's fine.'

****

We decided to leave after lunch from Ikhwan restauran .Their food was heavenly tested .We took coffee just after launch . This coffee is their own product , named "Kopi Ikhwan". But before a final decision could be taken nowhere we should go, Mr Khairuddin turned up   the idea. It was he who eventually settled the matter.

We decided to leave after lunch from Ikhwan restaurant . Their food was heavenly tested.

'I heard of the daylight crooked taxi drivers,' I said. 'Actually newly arrived foreign tourists are regularly approached at the bus stations by unlicensed car. Besides being illegal, this is potentially dangerous and you're pretty certain to be ripped off. Only get into an official cab, which will display the company name and phone number. If you're going to Pulau Perhentian, be aware that some taxi drivers, working on commission, will take you to the tiny port of Tok Bali on the southern coast of Kelantan instead of the main departure point of Kuala Besut. Several people. have complained about the reliability of the sole ferry operator in Tok Bali and I recommend you take a boat from Kuala Besut.' Said Mr Khairuddin.

I began to feel slightly uneasy. If Mr Khairuddin stayed for too long, our plans for the afternoon would be spoilt. But he asked at this point, 'Are you planning to go out or will you go back to hostel?

Philip said, 'Well, Rashed haven't seen anything yet. So I was thinking of taking him somewhere else.'

'Haven't you seen the Kelantan Kite Museum?' Mr Khairuddin

asked me. I shook my head.

'Then allow me to show it to you. You won't find a guide like me.   I have a thorough knowledge of the History of Kelantan....ha! ha! ha!'

All of us got into Philip's car. Philip and I sat in the front. As we were passing through Jalan Mutiara, Mr Khairuddin asked   us with a smile, 'Did you   ever think you'd get involved in such an event in Kelantan?' I shook my head. Philip chuckled.

Philip spoke this time. 'Rashed is thrilled to be here,' he said, 'because he's very interested in such things , you see.'

'Indeed?' Mr Khairuddin sounded both   surprised   and pleased, 'It's an excellent way of exercising the brain.

The wau   or   traditional kite   museum was really worth seeing. It was   at Pantai Sri Tujuh, 26 km from Kota Bharu, was a   complete   showcase   of   kite   culture, providing information on the history and development   of these giant kites. Moreover it   was   a   beautiful place—there were trees everywhere around this place. The museum has displays of the various types of kites, and also   teaches   visitors about the age-old traditions in Kelantan and other states in Malaysia, as well as traditional kites from around the world. Enthusiasts who was keen to learn were taught how to make decorative kites and fly them properly.

I had read about the capital, Kota Bharu, with its clutch of museums, vibrant cultural activity and tasty culinary specialties, was a great place to begin the exploration of Kelantan and also makes the perfect base from which to explore the surrounding country side made those events pass through my mind like pictures on a screen. Mr Khairuddin, in the meantime, had begun his commentary.

'By the 1820s Kelantan was the most populous and one of the most prosperous states on the Malay peninsula. As was the case in Terengganu, it managed to escape the ravages of the disputes that plagued the west-coast states, and so experienced largely unimpeded development . Also like Terengganu, Kelantan had strong ties with Siam (now Thailand) throughout the 19th century, before control was passed to the British following the signing of an Anglo-Siamese treaty in 1909. Kelantan's wealth and importance waned after the ties with Siam were cut, and as a northerly backwater of colonial Malaya the state declined. Kelantan was the first place in Malaya to be invaded by Japanese troops in WWII.

During the Japanese occupation, control of the state was passed to Thailand, but in 1948 Kelantan became a member of the Federation of Malaya!'

Philip had gone for a walk since he had seen the kite museum before. Only I was inside, totally engrossed in what Mr Khairuddin was saying, and looking at the museum has displays of the various types of kites. After seeing everything we began walking back to the car. Mr Khairuddin did speak to me again that day a lot of matter. When we got back into the Philip's car, it was only seven to five by my watch; but it was already dark. This surprised me since I knew daylight could not fade so quickly. The reason became clear as we passed the main road and came into the Pengkalan Chepa again.

Thick black clouds had gathered in the western sky. 'It generally rains at night,' informed Mr Khairuddin. 'The days here are usually dry.' We decided to drop Mr Khairuddin go back to the hostel as there was no point now in trying to see other places.

I did not utter a single word on our way back. Simply stared out of the car, was taking in everything to see. I know , If Mehbub went up this road again on a different day, I was sure he'd be able to remember the names of all the shops we saw. Would I ever be able to acquire such tremendous powers of observation, and an equally remarkable memory like Mehbub Anowar? Ididn't think so. On returning hostel, I spent most of my time either pacing up and down in the room or scribbling in my notebook.

CHAPTER 7

The next morning, by the time I got up, Philip had already gone outside. This surprised me, since I had no idea he was in such a hurry to go outside. My plans were different. I had wanted to spend the morning at hostel. Philip might have accompanied me. It had rained the night before and was still cloudy and kind of oppressive. So I decided to wait until Philip got back.

After two hours later Prof Dr. Youhan rang me. This must be telepathy, I thought. Because I was thinking of him. Before coming to Kelantan, I had often thought about my past adventures and wondered what had become of those people had exposed. Farid of Dubai, Asadurzaman Khan in Jessore - had they been adequately learnt their lesson? Or were they still out there somewhere, spinning more webs of crime? After all, they all had enormous cunning. Why, some of them had so nearly managed to

get away!

Prof Youhan car was waiting outside of the hostel .By the time I

reached there, it was almost one p.m. He greeted me with a

warm smile. We left immediately, and by a quarter to two, we

were in The Kelantan River -Sunga kelate in Kuala krai.

We were in The Kelantan River -Sunga kelate in Kuala krai.

'Do you know why the sight of river have such a refreshing effect on our mind?' asked Prof Youhan. 'The reason is that people, since primitive times, have lived with near by river all around them, so that their mind have developed a healthy relationship   with   their environment . Of course, river in big cities these days have become rather difficult to find. As a result, every time you get away from country, your mind beg into relax, and so does your eyes. It is mostly in cities that you'll notice people with depresses mind. Go to a village or a hill-station, and you'll hardly find anyone feeling depression.'

We came to a restaurant near to the river .He had a quiet dignity about him, and looked younger than his age.

I could see a lot of coconut trees as I took a chair.

'How did you find my article?' Prof Youhan asked.

'Very informative. Many things would have remained unknown to me if I hadn't been read your article.'

'The thing is, you see, I believe the five E - formula that is Energy, Effort, Enjoy, Enthusiasm, Excellent. You must know how to store your energy , if you have energy then you can give effort , but you must feel enjoy about your work then you get the enthusiasm , once everything is complete then you will get

the excellency. So I thought I'd try and do some thing worthwhile

before I died - after all, I am over fifty - and let my student know

how to do work properly' .

'When did you first start writing ?'

'Let me think…..yes, I came to Rome , to   attained in a

conference at 5 December 1993. That time from one of my

friend I had heard of my supervisor name Prof Dr John Brewster.

That time my friend had already done his PhD. He really had a

wonderful skill'.

'I   heard   there   was   some   mysterious   about   your

supervisor?'

'Yes ,I joined the Faculty of risk management in Rome

University. That was where I directly work under the supervision

of Prof Dr John Brewster. He came from an aristocratic family.

What many people didn't know was that he first published the

article about risk management from Rome University when he was

a PhD student.

When he was become my supervisor then it was not difficult

after this for me to learn many interesting things from   him. But one   day   he was vanished from his apartment. Still it was a great mystery about his suddenly vanished. Some said he was dead and some said he was kidnapped .But nobody discovered his body. Four years I worked on his supervision, but I could not complete my PhD because of his disappearance, then I came to my country and complete my PhD.'

'I have heard he had famous article of risk management?'

'Yes, but how much do you know about it?'

'Nothing at all. I've seen it in news, that's all. I think it was in somewhere   news   that   some   of   this   great manuscript was stolen'.

'Yes, you're right. He had many enemy .But it was no ordinary manuscript. It was probably the best known article in the last phase of his life'.

'Tx-6? But isn't it true that there aren't too many formula done after him?

'Yes. Most known theory were begun by him, and finished by others who worked in his Academy. Many scholar of those times worked like that. But this articleTx-6 bears every evidence of risk management. Prof Dr John Brewster showed it to me.'

'That would make it totally invaluable, wouldn't it?'

'That's right. If any journal find his unpublished article which was stolen and if they decided to sell it, it's difficult to say how much they might get. Seventy-five thousand dollars, perhaps. May be even more.'

Even so, many people came to you , because you was his best student .'

'One day an Armenian came to me. William Anderson. Stinking rich. Has a business in Singapore and is a collector of old unpublished manuscript. Said he had many original writing manuscript . He had heard from his friend that I happen to have worked with Prof Dr. John Brewster. He wanted to buy if I have any of his writing manuscript. Yes I had some , but I didn't sell, of course. Then he said he had read my article. He was bragging so much that when he began to ask me about the Tx-6 formula . Anyway I am fairly wealthy.

He then said he would get hold of that the manuscript by hook or by crook. So I thought…..but perhaps he had to go back to America on business. He has an agent here.' 'But that unpublished article of Prof Dr. John Brewster now belongs to his family.'

'Possibly yes , it could not be a public property , still nobody clearly knows he is still alive or not .However Prof Dr John Brewster too ashamed to speak of himself. Perhaps he's realized how disappointed his wife was with him - so much so that, in the end, he left his home, his career, everything. We used to have arguments about this.'

'Did he stay in touch with you?'

'Yes, he used to write to me occasionally. But I haven't heard from him for a long time now.'

The next day, Prof Dr. Youhan showed me everything worth seeing in the university - the Faculty, the Gardens, and the play ground. In the evening, he arranged to have me driven straight to his home. I had a good dinner of all his family members. I gave thanks for his wonderful hospitality.

'Mr Rashed,' he said, laying a hand on my shoulder, 'please work regularly.'

I reached hostel at around the night 11 a.m. that day. The phone rang almost immediately at morning. It was Prof Dr. Youhan calling from the university. 'Come here at once, 'he said urgently, 'there's some excellent talking about Research Methodology.'